A Poet's Dream

The Life Lyrics Of A Poet

Letina McDowell

A Poet's Dream

The Life Lyrics Of a Poet

Published by:
Ware Resources & Publishing
We are an all in one Resources
and Publishing Company!
1-888-469-4850 Ext. 2

For more information about Ware Resources, visit our
website: www.wareresources.com

IBSN: 978-0-9974404-0-9

LC Control No: 2016904831

Acknowledgement

Milton McDowell &
Ernestine McDowell

I love you with all of my
heart Mom and Dad. Thank
you for all you have
done for me.

Special Acknowledgement

Rest In Peace "EZZ"

On 12-26-14 an Angel came and took you away, away from this sinful world, from your pain, I know there were times when you felt like going insane, and your tears were falling like rain, but your smile was so bright, and your skin was so pure and so light, such an evil person took your life, took your life, gun wounds to your body, how could someone kill such a wonderful person, with such a big heart, I know this because yes, I knew you since you were a little boy, watched you grow from a child to a man, a man with two beautiful seeds, how dare someone left you on that hard, and dirty ground to bleed, they're going to suffer for what they did, took your life, took your life, yes that what they did, that was a hard time, and took time to even believe, let alone believe that you were gone, yes gone, but you're not alone, I cry because I can't hear your voice on the phone, I cry because I can't see your face, but your memories I will never erase, you were the life of the party, yes the party starter, a man who truly loved his "family", I'm missing a part of my heart, a part that will always belong to you, but I do know you are in a better place, yes in a better place, "Resting In peace"

Jimmy Marcel Powers
1986-2014

Table of Contents

A Poet's Dream

The Life Lyrics Of A Poet

With This Rose

With this rose,

I give you my heart,

I fell in love with you from the very start.

You are my sunshine on a rainy day. You bring me happiness in a sad day.

When I was feeling stressed, you remind me of how blessed I am.

When I'm tired, you give me your arms to rest, and with this rose, I give you my best.

No matter what happens I will love you no less,

You're one of the reasons why I smile; I love the way you love me.

I love all the things you do to help take care of me and together we make a great pair.

I learned to look over your flaws. In my eyes you're perfect just for me, your heart is big, you showed me that you don't have anyone other than me, so with this rose I give you me.

A Real Man

Every woman wants a real man, I mean a man that says he can,

I mean that knows how to put a smile on your face, in other words, know how to bring you joy,

I mean to treat you like a queen, in other words like y'all a team,

I mean that knows how to love you, even if y'all struggling, I mean to know how to make a hustle, in order to make a dollar to get through the struggle.

I mean to leave his boy so he can come home to you, so y'all can lay up, in other words, cuddle, and feel all over you up under the covers, because that's your best friend, in other words, that's your lover, a real man that will make sure his money is tight, just to get it right before creating a family, in other words, achieve his goals to take care of his family,

I mean go above and beyond and take chances, and on a good night, he will take you out for a few dances, and whisper in your ear and say I love you baby and thank you for giving me so many chances.

A real man will love you like no other, in other words when its time he will place a ring on your finger and make you his wife and love you for life.

A Sorrowful Small Town

This is so hard to say, but we live in such a small town and death is always in our way, every day we hear something bad that happened around our way. So many hearts are broken, so many of our young people are crying out for help, they don't understand why.

All they can do is scream and ask what's going on and why? Why are all our young people trying to be thugs and killing their own kind? All I can reply is I don't know young blood but use your own mind.

Stay out of trouble and stay away from the bad kind.

Stay motivated, work hard and cherish your time. Drop down on your knees and pray. Ask God to watch over you and your family and prepare you for a better day.

All this shooting and killing is driving our town insane, so many of our young people are using alcohol to cope with their pain, popping pills because that's the only way they know how to live, trying to be in a gang because they think that's a new thing, selling drugs because they want to be like those thugs.

Some of their parents are gone, and our kids are so confused.

My God, they've been mentally abused. God, I just want our kids to stay strong, just leave these streets alone,

Such a sorrowful town we live in, these street thugs took my cousin away,

Bullets to his back, they just blew him away, didn't care how he was left there to be put away, the snakes just took him away.

He thought those boys were his friends, but you see they brought his life to an end.

My God, my God, it felt like a dream, bad thoughts took over me, my family and friends were there for me.

My cousin's death was a wake-up call for me, so young people, older people, all of God's people, get your mind right, stay close to God, stay strong and never give up hope.

A Thin Line Between Love and Hate

A thin line between love and hate, it's a very thin line between love and hate. See I use to love him and hate him at the same damn time. One minute I was happy and the next minute I was sad. Yes I know that sounds bad, but that was the love and hate relationship that we had.

Mixed feelings that we shared, the way I felt when I was madly in love, can't be explained. See my feelings were all over the place, see the simple words he used touched my heart, it was easier said than done but I fell in love from the very start.

He was number one on my love chart but number 10 on my hate chart. I use to eat his words like a fish eating bait, then sometimes I just wanted to drown him in a lake, it's only so much a women can take, that's love and hate. There were a few times I imagined myself crying at his wake, it took me years to realize that he was a fake, but I still stayed, but I still stayed.

The line was so thin that I couldn't pretend, it was bad enough that I was living in sin. The words he said, yes made me love him; But the things he did, yes made me hate him. It was a thin line between love and hate.

Afraid To Love

Afraid to love, because love goes so deep down inside and has your mind open so wide, have your body feeling so weak, and your heart is broken for weeks and weeks, and you try to ease your mind, but every time you close your eyes all you can think about is the one who told you all those lies.

And all you do is cry and cry and cry, and that makes you afraid to love and give it another try,

And as you're wiping your face dry, you're thinking of all the times your mate made you cry, and you ask yourself why?

And as weeks pass by, you're trying to heal, trying to fix everything that was broken, but in your heart, you knew you were a token, trying to figure out where you went wrong, and you're trying to stay strong, but the people on the outside will not leave you alone.

They're trying to force you to give love another try, but you're afraid, afraid love is going to fail you in every way, so you choose to be by yourself every day in every way, then you know love can't fail you in any way, afraid to love.

But Still I Stand

But still I stand, anything is possible and yes I can.

My mind is strong, I'm not always right, sometimes I'm wrong, but I didn't get through my ups and downs alone,

My friends heard the same tone over and over, but still I stand.

There was a time in my life when I just ran away from my problems, but not one day passed me by when I did not pray.

I praised my God each and every day, and always kept positive people around my way.

There were as few snakes that hated me on the low, but my face still kept a bright glow, but still I stand.

There were days when I was stressed, days when I was depressed but my God loved me no less. I always tried my best to be my best.

There were times my hopes and dreams seemed unreal, there were times when I didn't think my heart would ever heal, but still I stand, and I'm proud to say yes I can.

Cherish Every Moment

Cherish every moment as if it's your last, not saying to forget about your past, but is good to live life and have a blast. We as people always complain about certain things, crying and complaining about the things we can't change, and crying and complaining about the things we can change. We need to get our minds right and think.

This could be our last day, but all we think about is having it our way, a lot of people don't live to see another day.

Think about the people who are sick or the loved ones we may have lost, so we need to take this time to cherish every moment with our family and friends and just love each other very deep to the end.

Learn to forgive and how to live, without being so stressed and learn to confess all the things that are on your chest, and then you will be able to get some rest.

Let go of the people in your life that are becoming a pest because life is too short.

We need to live everyday like it's a new start, don't carry so much hurt around in your heart, surround yourself with good people that want to see you do good, and help you out in times when they should.

That don't talk behind your back, and love you and you know that's a fact, somebody you can call and talk to when you up and down, and they're always around, that clowns around, makes jokes to make you laugh, and care less about your past.

Time always heals broken hearts and scares and teaches you how to face up to your fears. We as humans shed so many tears, and often we let other people control our mind, and that's what usually puts us in a bind.

You need to let loose and feel free to do what's best for you, cherish every moment as if it's your last, and treat every day like it's a new task.

When you start to cry, stop and think who made you feel like this and why.

And think this may be your last day, and you need to play this role in a different way, a role that makes you happy in every way.

Cherish every moment as if it's your last, now I'm done with this poem all those words are in my past.

Colors

Colors, our young people are dying over colors, trying to take over the world with colors, different gangs have their own color, but what if there were no colors.

You got the blood as red against the crips that're blue and neither one of these gangs have no clue about what the world is coming to.

Racism is all over, I mean black and white, whites don't like the blacks and blacks don't like whites.

What if there was no black and white, then what will we have not to like, you see Michael turned his color to white but what if black was white? Then would Michael have changed his color? Um, that's something to think about right.

Colors, all over the world we see so many different colors, but what if in all our eyes, we all see the same color's, then we'll be all lames because we see the same things, are will we all get along because we just the same?

So many people look at others and judge them by their color but the bible said we are supposed to love one another, but it's so hard to get along with each other, because no one is like the other, it is so crazy how people judge others because of their color.

Our skin may be different colors, but we are all human and no color is better than the other, so think about it, when you pick up a box of crayons, they're all different colors, but all in the same box beside one another.

Colors, we as people have different personalities, different mind frames, different styles, but if you look over your head, we all are seeing the same cloud, we all feel pain, we may not deal with it the same; when we bleed our blood is red that should be enough said, but instead, we judge by our color, yea by color.

It's not right but by our color, life is too short to think otherwise, we need to love one another and stop judging by our color.

A Story Of A Confused Child

I was introduced to this young boy. A boy that didn't even trust himself, he'd been mentally abused by so many, yes he'd been mentally abused by so many. He was so sweet but at the same time he had dark side; a side that just took over his pride. He said, "why, why did my mommy lie?"

He didn't know his dad and had a sorry ass mother. He'd been from place to place and the D. S. S. had to take his case.

This young boy couldn't understand why he wasn't in his mother's plan.

He was living on the streets, but he had a strong mind and believed in God.

Yes he was always in a bind but he was of a kind. He was such a confused child, but he had a heart of gold, and he was so bold. You got to have a heartless soul to leave your child out in the cold. At the age of eleven he started selling drugs, but he still never lived like a thug.

He was a young boy that had to take care of himself, it's not his fault that his mom left, no it's not his fault that his mom left, and his dad was sorry and just as bad.

His situation was so sad, I opened up my arms to this child. I listen to his story and wiped his tears as he cried. This young boy was so wise, his mom gave up a great prize. It was years later and too late before she realized, realized that she was dead in his eyes.

He said he use to sit and fantasize about having a childhood with his mother and father. He said my god reminded me that he was my mother and my father.

This young man prayed no matter where he stayed, he never gave up, that confused boy is now a man of god who achieved all his goals, he was once confused but he choose the right path.

Happy Mother's Day

Dear mama, I can't explain how much you be there for me, and all the love that you give to me when I think of you. I think of a falling star, because you always stayed up to par, and you and dad helped me get my first car, and when I moved away from home you see I didn't move very far.

You had three kids. I know it was rough, but we always had more than enough. You made a way every day; to make sure we were good in every way. I call because I have to hear your voice every day; it wouldn't be the same any other way.

You always speak your mind and keep it real and say what you have to say, and when I need something I can always get it on your payday, because you're my mama and you love me in every way.

You're a good wife, that's why dad made you his wife and promised to love you for life. You raised us to be independent. Even as a kid, you had us in the blueberry field and taught us how to take off tobacco. You made it fun and we didn't mind getting burned up in the sun.

I hate when you're mad, because then I feel so sad. Dear mama, the best mama, better than any other mama.

I love the Sunday meals you cook, you're the real deal, and the way you make those cakes, dang mama you will make anybody stay awake. I know I may be a pest but you still don't love me no less. I still remember when I was a baby, I use to lay on your chest, and hear you pray for us to have the best. I know you use to be mentally tired when you worked those two jobs, and you did it about all your life, so I thank god you retired, so now you can sit back and relax, take a few vacations and don't ever have to lack. You made our house into a beautiful home, and you will never be alone.

I love to hear you sing even though mama you can't hold a tone, but it's okay mama, you just put us in a zone. You like to joke around and make us laugh, even put on those crazy clothes and you know they don't match, but it's okay mama you're uncut, and that's what we like. You have five grandkids and three of them see you every night. They love to hear you fuss, and your daughter ain't never really heard you cuss, but anybody screw with us, you will put them in the dust. I love you mama and it's not lust, and you about the only one I can trust. I don't tell you everything but you know enough. But you been there every minute and that's enough. I can't ask for a better mama, I wouldn't trade you for the world and that's just being honest, so I just want to say I love you mama.

I Love Me Some Him

I love me some him, see his smile is what got me.

Then his eyes surprised me, his voice uplifted me.

I never believed in love at first sight until I met him.

I love me some him, we became so much more than friends.

He knew just how to ease my mind, he's always right on time.

The words he uses is all so kind.

People don't believe me but he's one of a kind, he's never left me in a bind.

Falling Star

Last night I was sitting outside my beautiful home looking up at the sky, questioning myself about my life, saying to myself I think I'm ready to be a wife. But deep down inside I love my life; it's not how I imagined it to be but it's just right for me.

As I sat outside on my steps looking up at the sky, I saw a falling star. It was falling slowly but seemed so far; I had time to think and make a wish.

As I closed my eyes, I felt a breeze, I felt so relaxed, and as I was making a wish it became true. I didn't ask for much just a peace of mind.

My home is where I clear my mind; yea my house is one of a kind.

Even though sometimes I am in a bind, God knows just how to ease my mind.

I gave this falling star a name and it's called "You just eased my pain." I use to hate the rain because it made me feel so sad, but I gave rain a new name and it's called "Joy." Now I feel up to par and it's all because of my falling star.

Forget That Man

I'm going to take it back when I was eighteen you see. I met a man that wasn't even in my plans. He did the finer things for me, like take me out to eat on shopping sprees and on vacations every other weekend. He made me feel like a queen you see, but then a few years went by and everything starting going down the drain. I started going insane, driving in the wrong lane because I was in pain. He even called me a bitch and hit on me a little. I took a whole lot of shit. I started smoking weed a little bit, so I was like forget that man. I don't need that man. This nigga played me you see, like I was nothing but a made to be. But when I realized it wasn't for me, I walk away so I could be free. This man wouldn't leave me alone, I was laying in the bed and he put five bullets to my head. Thank God I'm not dead. Now he's walking around on powder and looking a mess. He's like a bit stressed, fucked up in the game because now he's lame. Now I got myself together, I'm doing better. I'm an independent chick, got my own shit, make my own money on my own time and this man doesn't have a dime. He played me, he didn't make me; now men don't know how to take me. He's a hot mess and my shit's gravy, so I'm like fuck that man, I don't need that man, he's a bitch made man.

My Future Husband

In my hot tub, sipping on a glass of wine, yes he's my future husband.

I'm one of a kind, it don't take much for me, just some of your time. Your money is worthless but your love means the world.

I don't need diamonds and pearls, just a hug and kiss to show those other brothers what they missed.

When I'm down, just give me a kiss on the hand, and tell me we will get through it, yes we can. Just whisper in my ear and tell me about your future plans.

As I'm soaking in this tub full of water, my imagination goes so wild. It goes beyond the clouds, I see myself going down the aisle and we're both saying our loving vows.

Now I'm about to step out this water and wrap my body in this warm towel. I will patiently wait for you, my future husband, yes that's you.

Guilt

Yes, his guilt is what made him stressed. Yes he shed tears because he hurts deep down inside, and he felt pain because he had too much pride.

See his guilt is what made him tell all those lies. See my dad taught me how to read through a man and his lies because yes my dad is very wise. See he told me a man should treat me good, because yes I'm a prize.

My dad said don't give a man but so many tries, because yes if he loves you, he will love you until the day he dies, and I asked my dad why? Why do men lie? My dad said, "If you got to ask why, then baby you need to tell that man bye."

I said, "Yes dad the guilt is killing him," my heart won't let me be with him. See dad, I thought there was a bet-ter side to him, but he's full of lies and I don't want him beside me. I said yes dad I thought I knew this man; I use to walk in public and hold his hand.

We even talked about buying some land. Dad I should have done as you said and ran. All them days in the kitchen cooking and slaving, and washing all them dam pans; yes I can tell the guilt is destroying this man and all he wants is fame.

But hell, I didn't think he had no shame, and yes I learned to love from a distance because the close lust was hurting me. I started doing things and getting upset with myself. Yes, I was giving it my best, but the devil wouldn't let me rest.

I had so much anger on my chest, I started loving him less and less. His bitterness was making me depressed, his eyes were deceiving me, and the touch of his hand started to disgust me.

The sound of his voice was annoying me. His guilt helped me; yes, helped me to realize that he wasn't the man for me. I knew then it was time to let go.

Yes, this man was putting on a show. Yes, he was so confused he didn't know which way to go. I set my mind free and now I just want loyalty.

Happy Father's Day

Happy Father's Day to my dad. Anyone can be a father but it takes someone special to be a dad. You were in my life since day one and you never left my side. You showed me how a man should treat his lady and how a man should work hard to keep his lady. Years at a time, you made me mad but at the end of the day I'm glad because it made me who I am today. I respect you in every way and wouldn't trade you for the world; And the way you cut the two-step lol, you made up your own old school dance. You're the same man for all 33 years of my life and you're the true example of a real dad. I love you and Happy Father's Day dad!

Heart Broken

Have you ever been heart broken? Felt like you lost your last token? Your life consisted on you sitting around hoping, are trying to find different ways to cope, cope with your pain.

Felt like you were going insane, your past life flashed in front of you? You were so broken you gave up on your future; life seemed so lame, you found so many flaws with other people that came your way.

You felt like nothing would ever be right. You lost sight and couldn't imagine another true love, broken down so bad, all your days were teary and sad. All you wanted was to be loved so bad.

Didn't realize how good of a life you really had, you was always mad, couldn't find a reason to be glad, you felt like your life was over, you just wanted to make one wish on a four leaf clover.

Heartbroken, I said have you ever been heartbroken; you couldn't put the pieces back together? You rather sleep alone and listen to slow songs, and go riding and think about your love all the way home.

Drink a glass of wine just to unwind, or think about how stupid they were and put you in a bind.

You overlooked so many people that were all so kind, you was tired of people lying and you got tired of trying. You wanted to give up, now it's time for you to keep your head up, stay strong and never give up.

I Refuse, I Refuse

I refuse, I refuse to be anybody other than myself. I Refuse, I Refuse. I am who I am. I am proud of myself. I refuse to like the things you do, just because you want me to. I refuse to change my independence for you. I refuse, I refuse to respect someone that doesn't respect (his/her)self. I am who I am because that's the way God wanted me. I speak what's on my mind but at times, I feel like I've been too kind to people that don't even deserve my time.

I refuse, I refuse to be a helpless, a helpless human being. I refuse to walk around with a frown on this pretty face, a face with a smile that no one can erase. I refuse to be stressed; and the women that I am, I said the women that I am, I will love you no less.

I refuse to accept stupidity from anybody else. I refuse, I refuse to be used and abused. I will, I will use all my energy to focus on my dreams. I think, I think at times I'm misunderstood, but don't let my pretty skin and my pretty smile, and soft voice fool you. I refuse, I refuse to be mistreated by someone that doesn't deserve my company.

I am who I am Ms. Molly Poetic is who I am.

I Was Only Four

I was molested, I said I was molested; do you even want to know the rest? I'm the only one who can tell my story the best. I was only four; I said I was only four, a baby, and an innocent little girl. My mother left me with someone she thought she could trust, but he was a child molester, he was my baby sitter. I only remember one time, but only God knows how many other times. He was my first cousin, he was old enough to know better, but why didn't he do better, he was eighteen, I was four. I said he was eighteen, I was four, God the things he did to me behind those closed doors. I remember that one day like it was yesterday. He said, "Molly take off your clothes and lay on the floor." I was only four. I did as he said, I was a little girl and I was scared. He pulled down his pants, this disgusting man got on the floor beside me, I remember saying I want my Mommy, but then this man got on top of me; he pulled his penis out and rub it against me over and over. He was rubbing his penis on my vagina, he was touching my innocent body, I was a baby, and I was only four. I remember crying and he told me to be quiet. He said, "You will be ok." I was scared. He then was trying to force his self in me, then I heard a car, he quickly jump up, made me get dressed, he grabbed my arm and told me not to tell. I'm not even going to lie; I hope he burn in hell. It was my mom who pulled up in that car; she got off early that day. God sent her to save me. I told my mom everything this bastard did to me; I showed her where he touched me. I remember my mom crying and going after him. I don't know what happen, but I know he didn't go to jail for what he did to me. My God that man molested me; I can't believe he walked away free, and the sad part is he my cousin and he still tries to come around me. He thought I forgot what he did to me, but it still lives inside of me. I had nightmares on top of nightmares all my life of being raped. I dream about that day still and I'm 32, that was 28 years ago. I remember like it was yesterday. I dislike him in every way. It was so hard coming up because I thought every man was bad, and men disgusted me. The sad part is, I can't remember if he did that to me more than once. I may have been too young to remember. That part of my life just won't go away. I've been carrying it around inside of me for years and years. I hurt now even when I talk about it, and I think about all the girls around the world that have been molested and scared to tell. But don't be like me, molestation is a crime; God knows my cousin should have done some time. I still have this void and this hate in my heart, hell I was only four. When I see him now I can tell that he remembers what he did to me, the look in his eyes, the way he stared at me and till this day he disgusts me.

I try to keep the peace but it takes everything out of me not to tell my family what he did to me. I was sexually abused, I was only four, he was eighteen. I was messed up for a while, I can't believe this man molested me as a child, I don't wish molestation on a child.

If I Could Go Back

If I could go back, go back in time that is, I would be a better me. I would be that innocent little girl that lives deep down inside of me, yes the innocent girl that lives inside of me.

The pure, innocent girl that I remember way back then, when the thought of sex disgusted me, when the thought of kisses and a boy brought the shyness out of me.

Back in the day when I wanted to keep my body covered by showing no skin. Not me, not back then, if I could go back I would follow my high school dreams.

I would pursue the things that seem impossible at this point in my life, not saying that it's not possible. Sometimes I feel like I'm living in a dream, I feel like I wasted so much time. I feel like my life is passing by so fast, I feel like I can't keep up.

I feel like the devil is constantly after me. I feel like a part of my life is a game. Lord knows I get tired of doing the same things, my mind is telling me it's time for a change.

I said my mind telling me it's time for a change, my heart telling me that I been through too much pain, "STOP" "Rewind" it's time for a change.

It's time to move on.

If I could go back.

Wait a minute, I don't want to go back, back then I remember the times when I was going insane.

I started writing poetry to cope with my pain, back then the weakness came out of me.

I failed some test. I started writing poetry to cope with my pain, back then the weakness came out of me. I failed some test and passed some test but my

God loved me no less.

If I could go back, I would live for today. I said live for today.

In A Zone

I'm sitting here in a zone, thinking about all the things in my life that went wrong.

My list seems so long, but yet that's what made me strong.

Now that I'm grown, seems like time is passing by so fast.

I don't know how long these feelings will last. Every day I wake up with a new task, my mind is going in circles and my heart is beating really fast.

Nothing is promised, we don't know how long we going to last, or how long we going to be in this world and dread our past. But our future is the only thing that really matters, having hopes and dreams and strong minded people on our team.

I'm sitting here in a zone.

I just heard a voice speak to me in a soft tone saying you are not alone, saying yea you made mistakes but you learned how to confess up, so keep your head up, stay strong and never give up.

In Due Time

In due time, you will be mines, I say in due time. Because I choose to take my time, I want to learn everything about you before I make you mines.

I want to know your likes and your dislikes in due time. I will know everything that you like to do for fun. I hope you don't mind lying on the beach under the sun.

Sometimes I might call you boo and sometimes I might call you hun. My thoughts might even freak you out sometimes but don't you run. I want to learn to look over your flaws, and I want you to accept my flaws. We can be Bonnie and Clyde but I don't want to break no laws.

I will learn to love your child as my own, some days I may feel a bit stressed but hold my hand, don't leave me alone. In due time, I will learn your favorite song, I can't sing but I will play along.

I want to get in your head and be your thoughts. I want to be the reason for your smile, being single is fun, but the fun only lasts for a while. In due time, I will be ready to accept and be your queen, I want to be your best friend and then your lover.
In due time, you will be mines.

Innocent Love

Innocent love, have you ever had that innocent love? That love you had with someone and you know it was real, the love when you in pain and it made you heal? That love that gave you a reason to live, it had you feeling so high like you was up on a hill, or felt like you just popped a pill.

That love that makes your whole body tingle, that make you have an orgasm by the sound of the voice, that love that put a smile on your face that no one can erase, that love that makes your day go by smooth and put you in groove, that love that never went wrong, that love that's on repeat like your favorite song?

That love even from a distance you don't feel alone, that's that innocent love. That love that makes your heart race, and the gentle touch of their hand on your face, and the way their eyes looking when staring in your face?

That love they give that makes you feel so complete, and no one could ever compete.

That love that makes you feel so strong minded, that love that makes you change your bad ways, and gives you energy that last for days.

That love that will always keep ya'll together and you will never go separate ways?

That love that has that sweet smell, and you know your mate so well.

The kind of love that makes you kiss and tell; that love that gives you good thoughts.

That love that makes you take long walks and think about all the great talks.

That love that's not a game, that makes you want to tat their name?

That love when you're feelings mature and ya'll feel the same, and you both don't mind taking the blame for giving each other fame.

That love that never gets boring and ya'll sit and tell each other life stories.

That love that doesn't ever have you worrying, that love that makes you feel at peace, and no one will never break that bond that's that innocent love?

Life Isn't Easy

Life isn't easy, life is only what you make it to be; only if you open your eyes you really can see, and to really love is to know God is the key. We all go through our ups and downs, but get on your knees and pray and God will turn it around. People may play you and people may use you, but gives us a second round. Life isn't easy but as long as you're breathing it don't matter how people treat you, and if you can make a way to play, you can make a way to pray, because God loves us in every way.

Life isn't easy, I say life isn't easy, because we can make it harder than what it's supposed to be, so be careful and make the right choices and then you will see how good of a life it could really be. So treat people the way you want to be treated because no one wants to be mistreated. Life goes on with or without you, even though you may feel alone trust and believe that God is holding your hand and walking along with you. When you get angry and want to fuss with your mate just think, God let you breathe today and get on your knees and pray for a better day, because God loves us in every way.

Life isn't easy, I say life isn't easy, so put your trust in God and see how good of a life it could really be.

Live For Today

Live for today, because tomorrow's not promised. Life is too short, so live for the moment. Enjoy today and push your past out the way, because if tomorrow comes then it will be a better day. God loves us in every way, so we need to be happy and live day by day. Do something you never did before, go somewhere you never been, date someone you thought you would never date, and live for today.

Living for today is only making tomorrow a better day. Life goes on with or without you. Leave all that stress in your past. Forget about being depressed and get some peaceful rest.

Look over all the people that mean you no good, and cherish the people that love you at all times.

Have a day out with yourself.

Look in the mirror and smile.

Open your heart to that special someone, and make it worth your while, live for today.

Lost In Love

Have you ever been so lost in love, so lost you couldn't tell if you were going are coming? So lost you couldn't find your way back, you going around and around in circles and finding yourself in the same place, trying to ease your mind but you can't because you got yourself in a bind?

So lost that your sense of direction is fading away, time is moving so fast, you going insane day by day, wishing these hurtful nights will go away? So lost that you having stomach pains because you can't eat and your head hurts from thinking too much? Feel like somebody threw a blow right to your gut, feeling pain in your butt for sitting down too much? You're carrying a frown and you know that's not how you get down, you in your zone and you don't want to hear a sound?

So lost your heart won't stop pounding, you got the shakes, and in your head you wondering how love makes you feel that way, and you want to sleep all your problems away but you know when you wake up it's going to be the same way because real love just doesn't go away?

So lost, all you can do is pray, everybody you talk to seem like a stray?

So lost that your tears are starting to feel weird, hitting on walls, walking back and forth through your halls, screaming love, love go away and come back in a better way, you trying to forget about your past but you know it won't last?

So lost your foot is pressing the gas but your mind is on overload, wishing someone will pick you up and take off that heavy load that's on your chest and maybe then you can get some rest because it's taking you so long to past this hurtful test?

So lost that when you close your eyes, you see all those roads running together, don't know which way to turn, and thinking in your head whether you'll ever learn, but all you can think about is making a U-turn because your love is so real and you don't want to give up, but in reality, you're fed up?

Um, it's time to give up and find your way back, back

to reality and lost in love.

Mirror

Mirror mirror on the wall, in your pocket book and even in the mall. You see the reflection of you that means you should love yourself just the way God created you. When you look in the mirror ask yourself Is what I'm about to do today a good decision that's going to reflect on me today? If the answer is no, then you need to make a better decision the following day. See, when things don't always go your way, just remember tomorrow is going to be a better day.

Mirror mirror on the wall, in your pocketbook and even in the mall. When you look in the mirror smile at yourself. When you look in the mirror say I am the one God created and I know he will never turn his back on me because I am the reflection of me. When you look into your eyes in the mirror, your eyes tell a story about you, and your story is even deeper when you're cry. When you look in the mirror at the reflection of you, search deep within you, and I promise you will bring out a better you.

Mirror mirror on the wall, in your pocketbook and even in the mall, different mirrors always going to show the same reflection of you.

The Perfect Man For Me

A man that loves God. Yes, I said a man that loves God. A man that shows respect as well as me giving him respect, a man that don't mind telling the truth even when it hurts, a man that has goals in life, and one day chooses to make me his wife.

A man that works hard everyday, and doesn't mind paying bills where he lay. A man that knows how to compromise and never cover up his life with lies; an honest man, one who will never deny me, but knows he can always rely on me. A man who is romantic and loves the finer things in life, a man who don't mind caressing my body after a long day at work, a man who overlooks my wrong, we can talk about it and move on. That's a part of being grown.

The perfect man for me, a man that might not know how to cook, but for his lady he will learn and study in some cookbooks.

A man that likes to spend quality time and know how to wine and dine,

A man that can get past my flaws and love me for my inner beauty and my outer beauty, a man that sees the good in me and pushes me to be a better me.

The perfect man would be the one who understands my fears, and will be there for me for years and years, and hold me when I'm in pain and shedding tears.

A man who can make me feel safe on a bad day, a man I can look in the eyes and I know he loves me in every way,

A man who likes to make love, knows how to do it gently and take his time. A man that needs and only wants me, and doesn't mind changing for the better for me.

A man who loves to hear me read my poetry and sit with me and talk about what my next move might be.

A man that treats me like a queen and yes that will be my king, that's the perfect man for me.

The Reason Why I Smile

The reasons why I smile;

I smile because I'm blessed. I'm blessed because I'm living; I'm blessed because I'm not stressed.

I'm blessed because I passed every test that the devil threw at me. I'm blessed because I have a family that loves me. I'm blessed to have a job so that I can take care of me.

I smile because I love me. I smile because God showed me how to be a better me, and to help people understand me.

I'm blessed because I have true friends that really care about me. I smile because I love seeing other people smile.

My smile is something no one could ever take away from me; my smile stays the same everyday.

When I smile, I hear people tell me I just made their day by the beautiful smile on my face.

My smile so bright because I try my best to do right, and I know one day my life going to be just right.

It feels good to smile because several times in my life I couldn't smile. Behind my smile is the inner beauty inside of me, that makes people love me.

I smile because God protects me. I smile when I think of how my future life's going to be. Right now to me it seems like a dream, but I smile because I'm working towards my dreams.

I smile because I'm happy. I'm happy because of the great life that was given to me, so thank you God for loving me, and giving me this beautiful smile that shows the better side of me, smile.

My Story

Once upon of time, I was once lost, I was once stressed out to the max, I was once broken, I was once scared, I once had low self-esteem, I didn't even know myself, yes that girl was me. I had to find myself because at one point my mind had left. There was a time in my life where it felt like I had nothing left. I felt lost because it took me so long to find my way back, find my way back to reality.

I had to get my mind under control, but the stress was taking over me, my mind was going blank over and over. I mean, I couldn't eat, I couldn't sleep, and things were getting deep. On one of my worst days, somebody robbed me for my jeep. I learned then that there are some things you just can't keep. But that was a little steep, it was like everything that was once whole, was broken. Now I can laugh like it was a joke because I was once scared, scared to go out the house and having nightmares. I had my support team, people who cared, people who listen to me and didn't mind how many times I shared my story. They were there for me, even when I felt there was nothing left inside of me. I wonder how I could let my heart get so heavy, and let negative thoughts take over me.

But it was just the devil trying to control me, my self-esteem was low, back then I couldn't put on a show. I couldn't even smile on the low, the only thing I could do was fall on my knees and say "God, please, help me through this heartache and pain."

Lord stop me from going insane, I need to get it together and stay in my lane.

I've been going through for so long, I'm starting to feel ashamed like this was all a big game.

Lord touch my heart and help me to a new start. Help me change my bad ways, and prepare for better days. That was my prayer, and it was answered in every way. Now I'm living my life in a happier and healthier way, and down on my knees, I will stay; Because it feels so good to pray in every way and I make it my best to pray every day, that's my story.

What My Heart Desires

My heart desires a man who loves me for my inner beauty and my outer beauty, loves me when I'm doing good or bad, loves me more when I'm sad as well as when I'm mad.

My heart desires a man that loves me when I tell him how I feel so I can see if he's the real deal.

My heart desires a peace of mind, to know that when you're gone you feel my love and your mind goes into a zone; and when I leave you home alone, you know I'm coming back. No worries, no stress because our love is a fact. To know when you're chilling with your friends, you're still coming back, because I'm the women you're with and will always have your back.

My heart desires trusts because without trust you have nothing but lust and lust turns into rust. Because there is nothing left, trust is a strong word that makes two people fall in love, make you feel like you got wings and can fly away like two strong doves.

My heart desires that unconditional love, like on a Sunday morning when the preacher speaks. It goes in so deep, because I know you're the one I want to keep, and you ask me what my heart desires?

My heart desires a special man that doesn't have to ask what my heart desires, so if you're the man for me, you will learn what my heart desires.

"Men"tally Abused

I once was that girl that was mentally abused.

I use to hurt so bad, so deep down inside and wonder how a man could use me, hurt me and lie so damn bad, but yet I was the one feeling so damn sad.

I use to have low self-esteem and felt like I had nobody on my team. I use to be that one that fell so deep, thinking in my head, this that man I want to keep.

The way I use to cater to a man, I mean straight wait on man and believe it or not I was straight down for my man.

I was such a good girl, I mean straight 100 percent with my man, but in his mind he had it all set up just to put me in a bind.

I mean like he was the only one I could get with, played me, I mean straight traded me, and all that time he stated to me that he wanted to be with me and proposed to me.

Even though I felt the answer should have been no;
I said yes, because I felt that one day
we would be blessed.

I knew not to settle for less, but every night I laid on this nigga's chest; I felt safe and got so much rest, but now I see it was all a test.

Just about everything he asked of me was always a yes, but then he became to be a pest.

When I told him no, he put on such a fucked up show and made me feel so low; sometimes I felt I was moving a bit slow.

I put on such a good show, that the outside of me showed a bright glow, until I realized he didn't really love doe.

I shed so many tears and had so many restless nights, this man just didn't know how to do right. I was mentally abused, I say again I was mentally abused by a man and felt so used. My family and friends had no clue what the fuck I was going through.

I'd been cheated on and left at home all alone. He was so selfish and he didn't even answer his cell phone.

He liked to fuck around and what's crazy is he did it in his own town, and he wondered why I always frowned when he was around.

He was a man that half way put in work, but still thought our relationship would work, then this man decided to move out of town.

I thank God he left and is not around, because it feels good that I don't have to look at this man when I ride around town.

No matter how good I was to this man, no matter how much I was there for this man, I realized you can never really please a man, but what I learned is to say fuck a no good man.

I've been mentally abused, I say I've been mentally abused and felt so used.

About The Author

Letina McDowell

Letina McDowell is the author of this life revealing written collection. Since the early age of 15, she has demonstrated a work ethic of a true lover of words and expressions. It was in high school when she started placing her thoughts on paper and it wasn't until more recently that she decided to share her poetry with the world.

She was born and raised in Fairmont, North Carolina where she graduated from Fairmont high school in 2000. In 2004, Letina realized her passion for working with children. She entered the mental health field where she works today and has earned various certificates over the past 12 years. In this work, the author has blended her true life experiences with her creativity and has created a heartfelt cuisine of emotions.

You are especially invited to join the talented Letina Mc-Dowell as she takes you into her world of poems based on true life stories.

WARERESOURCES AND PUBLISHING

WE ARE AN ALL IN ONE

ONE STOP PUBLISHING COMPANY!!!!

W.R.P. is a modest but skillful and knowledgeable Christian Publishing Company. We specialize in getting au-thors into print. We embrace and guide each author like a member of our family. We treat you fairly and recognize the importance of building a lasting relationship with you as an author. Join us in the walk to promote prosperity along with the message of encouragement and peace. Be one of the authors we transform and prepare for the world of information and books.

FEEL FREE TO CONTACT US@

www.wareresources.com

1-800-469-4850 EXT. 2

http://www.facebook.com/pages/
Ware-Resources-and-Publishing